To Grandm... House W...

Written and Illustrated by
Lawrence DiFiori

A GOLDEN BOOK • NEW YORK

Western Publishing Company, Inc., Racine, Wisconsin 53404

Cindy is on her way to visit her grandma and grandpa.

Cupcake goes along, too.

There are fluffy clouds in the sky and birds in the air.

Cindy can see Grandma and Grandpa's house through the trees.

Red and yellow leaves
fall down.

Let's play in the leaves!

Cindy smells something.
Cupcake smells something, too.

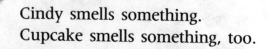

Now Cindy sees smoke and fire.
Someone is burning leaves.

It's Grandpa! Grandpa is burning the leaves.

Grandpa is happy to see Cindy
and Cupcake.

Cindy and Grandpa watch the fire.

The burning leaves smell good in the crisp air.

Cupcake smells
something else.

Cupcake smells Grandma's
pumpkin pie.

Grandma is very happy
to see Cindy.

The pumpkin pie is for
Cindy to take home.

Grandma pours apple juice for
Cindy and Grandpa.
Leaf burning makes you thirsty.

Cupcake is thirsty, too.

It is beginning to rain.
Cindy will have to hurry home.

Cupcake is hungry, too.

Don't forget Grandma's pumpkin pie, Cindy!

Good-bye, Grandpa!
Good-bye, Grandma!

Good-bye, Cindy and
Cupcake! Come and visit
us again.

Cindy and Cupcake run home.

That was a nice visit to Grandma
and Grandpa's house.
Now it's time for dinner and
Grandma's pumpkin pie.